All by myself!

For my mother, Dominique,
and my grandparents
Jeanne and Jacques
—Géraldine

For my parents
—Coralie

Owlkids Books Inc.
10 Lower Spadina Avenue, Suite 400, Toronto, Ontario M5V 2Z2
www.owlkids.com

North America edition © 2011 Owlkids Books Inc.

Text © 2010 Géraldine Collet
Illustrations © 2010 Coralie Saudo
Translation © 2011 Sarah Quinn

Published in Quebec under the title *Tout Seul!* © 2010
Éditions Les 400 coups, Montreal (Quebec), Canada
www.editions400coups.com

Distributed in Canada by University of Toronto Press
5201 Dufferin Street, Toronto, Ontario M3H 5T8

Distributed in the United States by Publishers Group West
1700 Fourth Street, Berkeley, California 94710

Library and Archives Canada Cataloguing in Publication

Collet, Géraldine, 1975-
    All by myself! / by Géraldine Collet ; illustrated by
Coralie Saudo ; translated by Sarah Quinn.

Translation of: Tout seul!
ISBN 978-1-926973-12-8

    I. Saudo, Coralie II. Quinn, Sarah III. Title.

PZ10.3.C64Al 2012   j843'.92   C2011-905819-7

Library of Congress Control Number: 2011935957

  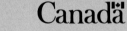 

Canadian Heritage — Patrimoine canadien

Canada

Ontario — Ontario Media Development Corporation — Société de développement de l'industrie des médias de l'Ontario

Canada Council for the Arts — Conseil des Arts du Canada

ONTARIO ARTS COUNCIL — CONSEIL DES ARTS DE L'ONTARIO

We acknowledge the financial support of the Canada Council for the Arts, the Ontario Arts Council, the
Government of Canada through the Canada Book Fund (CBF), and the Government of Ontario through
the Ontario Media Development Corporation's Book Initiative for our publishing activities.

Manufactured by WKT Co. Ltd.
Manufactured in Shenzhen, Guangdong, China, in October 2011
Job #11CB2494

A   B   C   D   E   F

 Publisher of Chirp, chickaDEE and OWL
www.owlkids.com

All by myself!

A story by
Géraldine Collet

Illustrated by
Coralie Saudo

When **Mama left**
the chicken coop
to go pecking for
grain, she left me
all by myself.

So I **cried.**
Just like Ivan
and Lily
and Leonard
and Shirley.

Ivan said our
mothers would be gone
for a **long time.**
"At least until **lunch,**"
thought Lily.

"What if they don't come home before it gets **really dark?**" worried Leonard.

ver!

wailed Shirley.

So I got
scared.
Just like Shirley
and Leonard
and Lily
and Ivan.

"What will we do
if they don't come back?"
I asked.

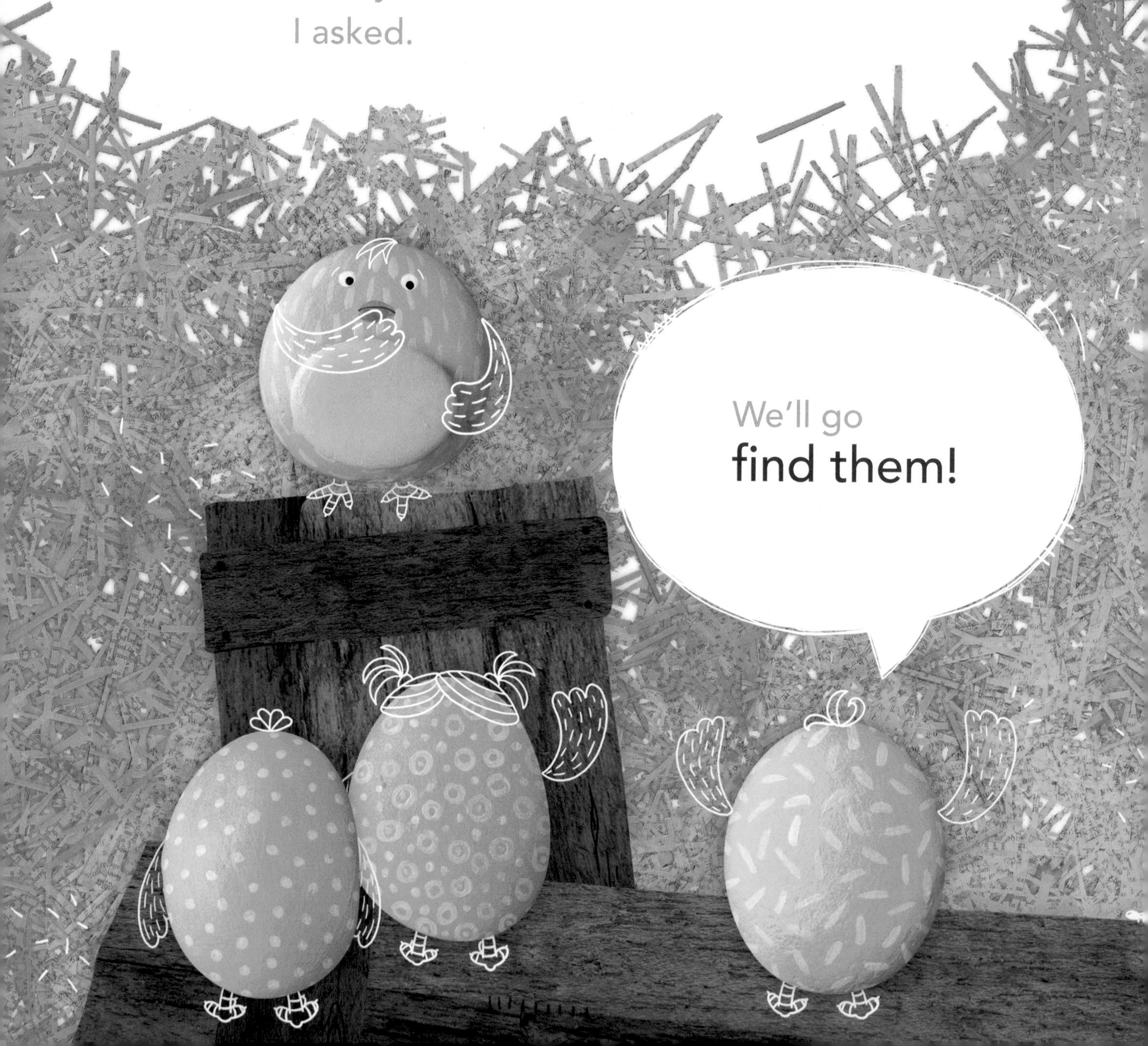

"Or just **wait here** until someone comes to help us," said Lily calmly.

The fox

"And what if it's **a fox** who **comes?**" asked Shirley.

Then Leonard began to hear **strange noises…**

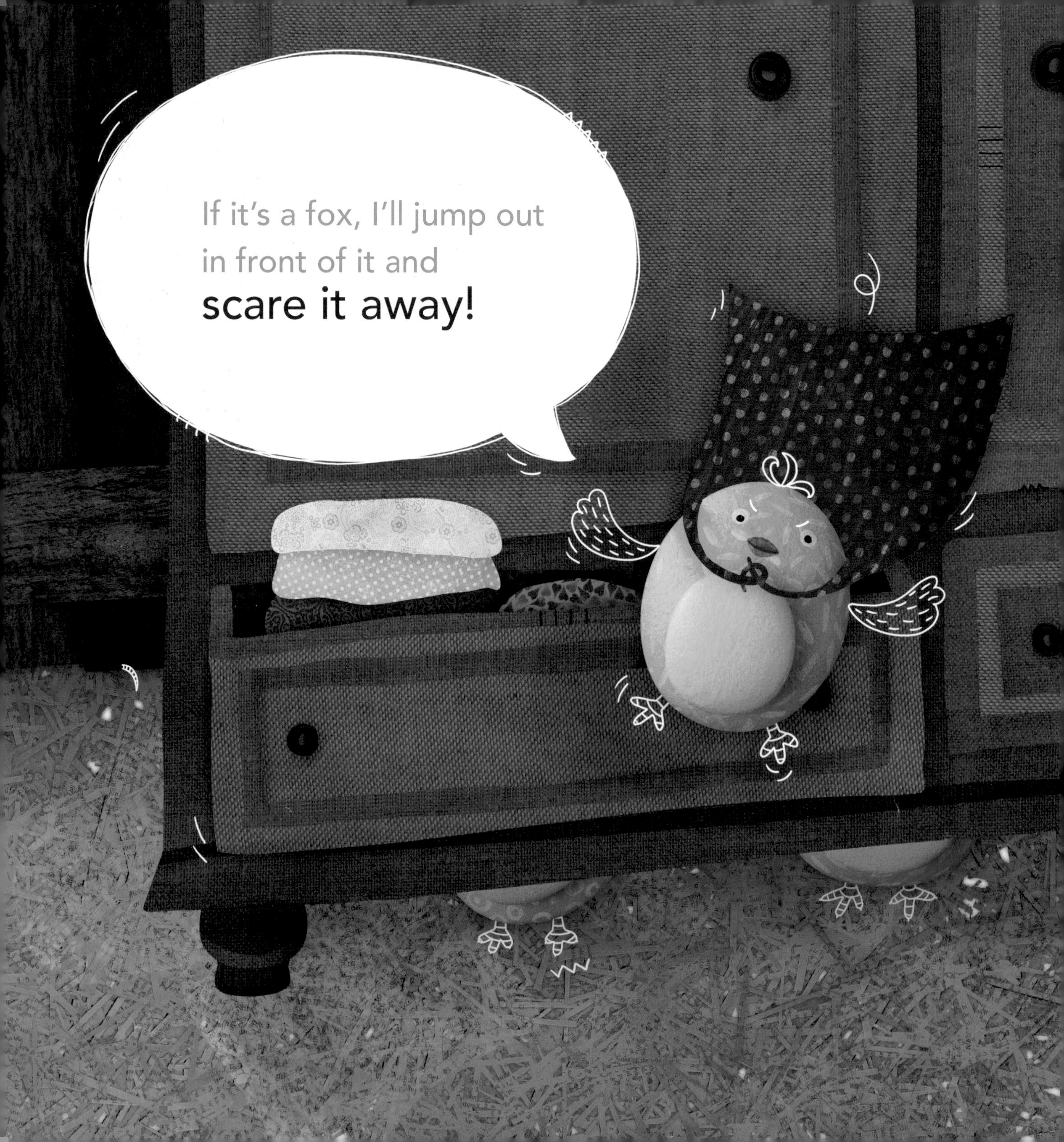
If it's a fox, I'll jump out in front of it and **scare it away!**

Oh no you won't,
you're too small…
If it's a fox,
we'll all hide
under the cupboard…

"There's not enough **room!**"
Leonard replied.

"I can't take it anymore!"
shrieked Shirley.
"He's going to eat us alive!"

Stop it,
Shirley!

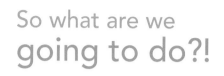

"I know!

Let's play a game. Whoever catches me **wins,**" Ivan shouted.

Then suddenly the **door** opened...

"We're home! Come, little chicks, who wants some nice grain?"

Our **mothers** came back! Hooray!

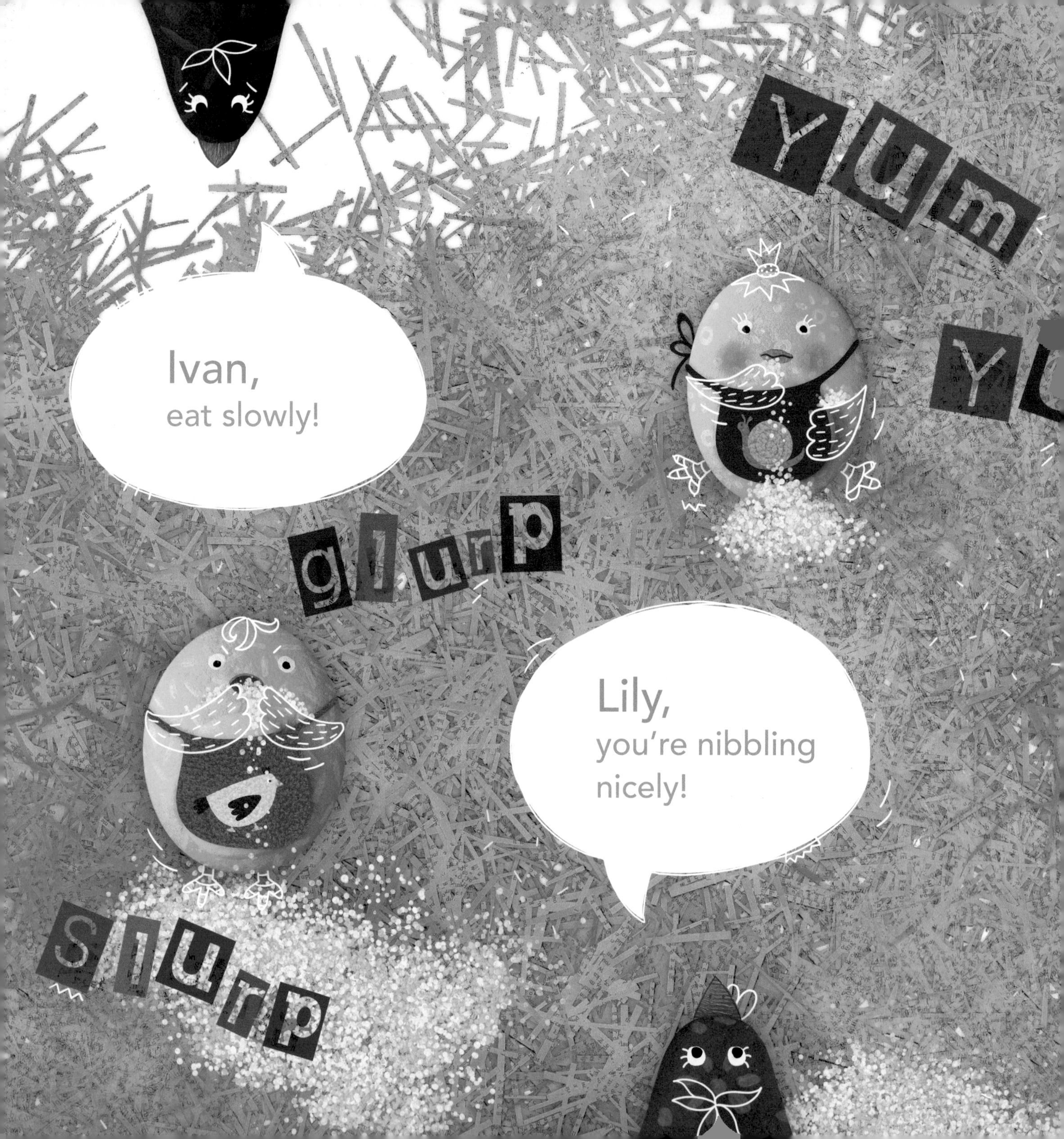

Ivan, eat slowly!
yum
glurp
Lily, you're nibbling nicely!
slurp

Hee-hee

Leonard, put your bib back on!

Shirley, chew carefully!

HOP HOP HOP HOP

"Anthony, do you want some help?"

"**No!** I want to be
just like Ivan
and Lily
and Leonard
and Shirley..."

"I want to eat
all by myself!"